A. A. MILNE

Winnie-the-Pooh's Baby Book

WITH DECORATIONS BY
ERNEST H. SHEPARD

Dutton Children's Books
NEW YORK

Hushed

"Hush!" said Christopher Robin turning round to Pooh.

"Hush!" said Pooh turning round quickly to Piglet.

"Hush!" said Piglet to Kanga.

"Hush!" said Kanga to Owl, while Roo said "Hush!" several times to himself very quietly.

Winnie-the-Pooh

The Story Begins

In Which We Are Introduced To

____

Born on ____________ at ____________

Place ______________________________

Doctor / Midwife ______________________________

Weight ______________________________

Length ______________________________

Color of hair ______________________________

Color of eyes ______________________________

ATTACH BABY'S FIRST PHOTOGRAPH HERE.

A Family Name

Next to Piglet's house was a piece of broken board which had: "TRESPASSERS W" on it. When Christopher Robin asked the Piglet what it meant, he said it was his grandfather's name, and had been in the family for a long time. Christopher Robin said you *couldn't* be called Trespassers W, and Piglet said yes, you could, because his grandfather was, and it was short for Trespassers Will, which was short for Trespassers William. And his grandfather had had two names in case he lost one—Trespassers after an uncle, and William after Trespassers.

Winnie-the-Pooh

A Very Fine Name

In Which We Learn More about Baby's Name

ATTACH BIRTH ANNOUNCEMENT HERE.

For the Record

In Which Baby's Important Things Are Stored

ATTACH BABY'S BIRTH CERTIFICATE HERE.

A Residence of Great Charm

In Which We Make Note of Baby's First Home

Address ____

____

____

First Visitors

____

____

____

____

____

____

ATTACH PHOTO OF BABY'S FIRST HOME HERE.

Rabbit's Family

"Suppose *I* carried *my* family about with me in *my* pocket, how many pockets should I want?"

"Sixteen," said Piglet.

"Seventeen, isn't it?" said Rabbit. "And one more for a handkerchief—that's eighteen. Eighteen pockets in one suit! I haven't time."

There was a long and thoughtful silence . . . and then Pooh, who had been frowning very hard for some minutes, said: "*I* make it fifteen."

"What?" said Rabbit.

"Fifteen."

"Fifteen what?"

"Your family."

"What about them?"

Pooh rubbed his nose and said that he thought Rabbit had been talking about his family.

"Did I?" said Rabbit carelessly.

Winnie-the-Pooh

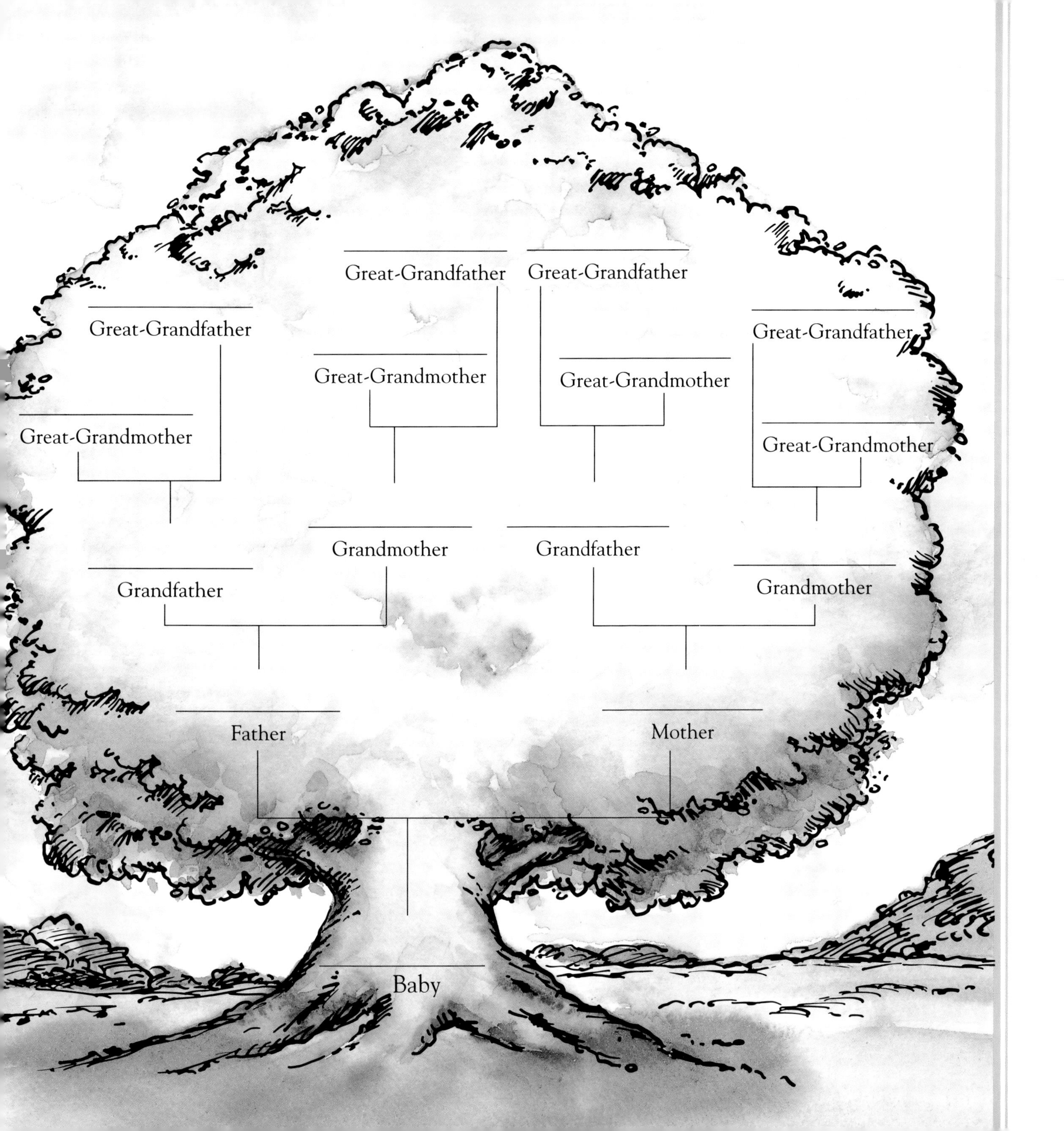
Great-Grandfather
Great-Grandfather
Great-Grandfather
Great-Grandfather
Great-Grandmother
Great-Grandmother
Great-Grandmother
Great-Grandmother
Grandmother
Grandfather
Grandfather
Grandmother
Father
Mother
Baby

The World as It Was

In Which We Make Note of Current Events

Headlines ______________________________

____

____

____

Political figures ______________________________

____

____

____

Books ______________________________

____

____

____

Plays ______________________________

____

____

____

Films

Fashions

Songs

ATTACH NEWSPAPER CLIPPINGS OR OTHER MEMORABLE ITEMS HERE.

A Party for Me? How Grand!

In Which Baby Is Welcomed

Ceremony date ____

Place ____

ATTACH PHOTO OF BABY HERE.

Friends-and-Relations

In Which We List Those Who Attended

A Very Small Animal

In Which Baby Grows and Changes

Age	Weight	Height
1 month		
2 months		
3 months		
4 months		
5 months		
6 months		
7 months		
8 months		
9 months		
10 months		
11 months		
12 months		

Sneezles and Wheezles

In Which We List Immunizations and Visits to the Doctor

Pediatrician ______________________________

Immunization	Date

Illnesses

____

____

____

____

____

____

____

____

____

____

His Teeth Are Rather New

In Which We Record the Arrival of Baby's Teeth

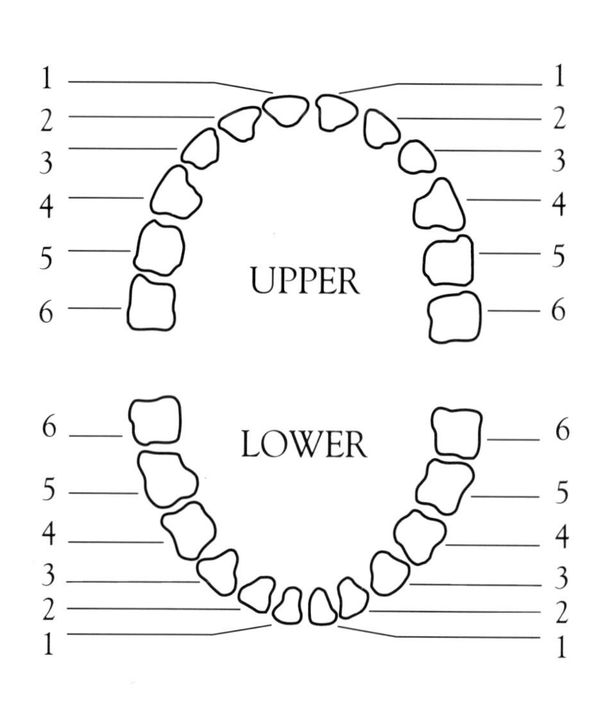

Tooth	Age	
1 central incisor	*7½ months*	________
2 lateral incisor	*9 months*	________
3 cuspid	*18 months*	________
4 first molar	*14 months*	________
5 second molar	*24 months*	________
6 first permanent molar	6 *years*	________

Tooth	Age	
6 first permanent molar	6 *years*	________
5 second molar	*20 months*	________
4 first molar	*12 months*	________
3 cuspid	*16 months*	________
2 lateral incisor	*7 months*	________
1 central incisor	*6 months*	________

Binker

Binker isn't greedy, but he does like things to eat,
So I have to say to people when they're giving
me a sweet,
"Oh, Binker wants a chocolate, so could you give
me two?"
And then I eat it for him, 'cos his teeth are rather
new.

Now We Are Six

Expotitions

In Which Baby Goes Out

Very Grand Things

In Which We Record Baby's Firsts

The first time Baby

had a bath ______________________

smiled ______________________

rolled over ______________________

laughed ______________________

crawled ______________________

slept through the night ______________________

sat up ______________________

stood ______________________

had a haircut ______________________

wore shoes ______________________

walked ______________________

spoke ______________________

drank from a cup ______________________

waved bye-bye ______________________

had a baby-sitter ______________________

grabbed something ______________________

recognized your name ______________________

ate solid food ______________________

used a spoon ______________________

cut a tooth ______________________

STORE CUTTING
FROM BABY'S FIRST
HAIRCUT HERE.

Gaiety, Song, and Dance

In Which Baby Celebrates Holidays

Baby's first holiday ____________________

____

____

Those with whom we shared it ____________________

____

____

ATTACH HOLIDAY PHOTO OF BABY HERE.

Other Holidays

King John's Christmas

"I want some crackers,
    And I want some candy;
I think a box of chocolates
    Would come in handy;
I don't mind oranges,
    I do like nuts!
And I SHOULD like a pocket-knife
    That really cuts.
And, oh! Father Christmas, if you love me at all,
Bring me a big, red, india-rubber ball!"

Now We Are Six

A Little Smackerel of Something

In Which We Learn Some of Baby's Favorite Things

Foods

Books

Toys

Stories

Playmates

Colors

Songs

Activities

"And we must all bring Provisions."
"Bring what?"
"Things to eat."
"Oh!" said Pooh happily. "I thought you said Provisions."

Winnie-the-Pooh

Amusements and Mishaps

In Which We Record Funny Stories and Minor Bounces

"When you wake up in the morning, Pooh," said Piglet at last, "what's the first thing you say to yourself?"

"What's for breakfast?" said Pooh. "What do *you* say, Piglet?"

"I say, I wonder what's going to happen exciting *today*?"

Winnie-the-Pooh

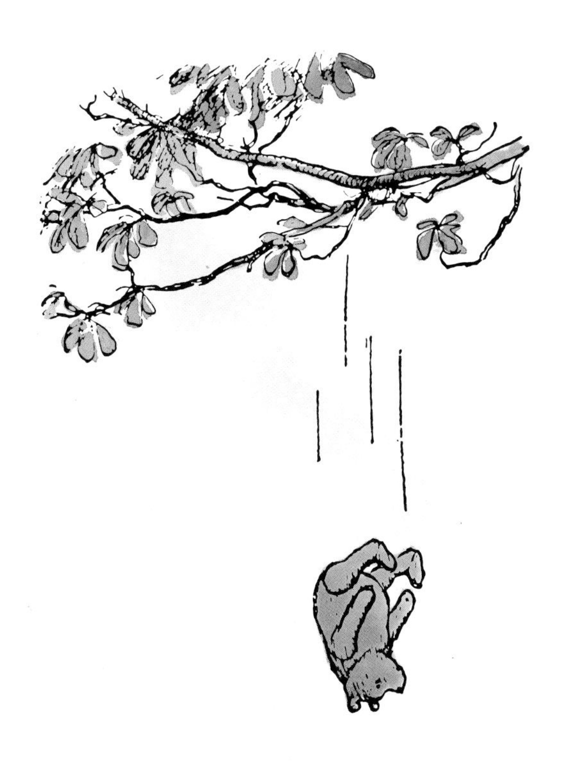

Eeyore whispered, "They're funny things, Accidents. You never have them till you're having them."

The House At Pooh Corner

Many Happy Returns

In Which Baby's First Birthday Is Celebrated

The Party ______________________________

____

____

____

____

____